LAURA OWEN & KORKY PAUL

Winnie AND Wilbur

Nitty WINNIE

OXFORD
UNIVERSITY P[...]

CONTENTS

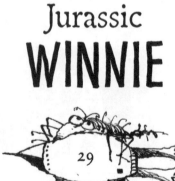

A Wedding for
WINNIE

Nitty
WINNIE

WINNIE'S
Wet Weekend

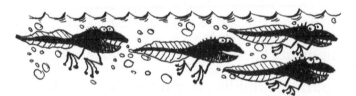

Plip! Plop! Water drip-dropped down from Winnie's ceiling. **Slosh!** Winnie's wellies waded ankle-deep through the water and **slap-splash!** her broom-mop squelched water into a bucket.

'Oh, soggy blooming sausages!' moaned Winnie. 'We'll have to start building an ark soon, Wilbur!'

'Mrrow,' agreed Wilbur, shivering on a high-up shelf.

'I hope Jerry can mend our leak soon,' said Winnie. 'Or we'll all get flushed out of the house just like . . .'

Wallop!-clongggg! went Jerry's mallet on the water tank upstairs, and moments later—**sloossh!**—water came pouring, tumbling down the staircase. It was now up to Winnie's knobbly knees.

Croak! said a happy frog who was gazing up at Winnie. **Splish-splosh** danced tadpoles like mini dolphins. **Swish-slither** swam an eel towards Winnie.

'Eeek!' Winnie scrambled up to join Wilbur on the shelf. **Creak!** went the shelf because it wasn't built for the weight of witches. 'Well, that's it!' said Winnie, as the shelf tipped them both—*splash!*—into the flood. 'If I'm going to wade in water and shrivel my toes to raisin-wrinkles, I'd rather wade and shrivel in warm water and in the sunshine.

Maybe even licking a nice-cream! Let's go to the seaside!'

'Meeow!' agreed Wilbur. He didn't much like the wet sea, but he did like sunshine and nice-creams.

So Winnie waved her wand.

Abracadabra!'

And instantly they were at the seaside.

'Ah!' sighed Winnie, kicking off her wellies and tucking her dress into her knickers. 'Just look at that sea sparkling like a beetle's back!'

'Mrrow,' scowled Wilbur.

'You're right,' said Winnie. 'I've had enough wetness for today, too. Let's make a sandcastle instead.'

They dug a moat and threw all the
sand into the middle to make a big castle
mound. Then they shovelled sand into
Winnie's hat, and upended it to make
turrets. They used Winnie's wand to
scrape door and window shapes, and they
slapped on shells to make it all look lovely.

'There! As pretty as a ferret in fairy wings!' said Winnie. 'I reckon we've earned ourselves a lice-lolly!'

They couldn't decide which flavour lice-lollies to choose, so they had four each . . . which meant a lot of fast licking— *slurp slurp!*—and sticky paws. Then they used the lolly sticks to make a drawbridge over the moat.

14

'Ah!' sighed Winnie. 'I'd love to be a princess living in our castle instead of a witch living in a flooded house. D'you know, Wilbur, I think . . .' Winnie picked up her wand.

'Meeeow!' Wilbur leapt to grab the wand from Winnie's hand to stop her from waving it. But he was too late.

Abracadabra!

15

Winnie was a princess. A very very tiny princess, just the right size to fit into their sandcastle.

'Mrrrow!' said Wilbur, trying to catch her as if she was a mouse. But tiny Princess Winnie had picked up her skirts and run over the drawbridge and into the castle before he could stop her.

16

'Oh!' said Winnie as she looked around.
'Oh, how princessy!'

There were seashell dishes and cups
on a table sculpted in the sand. There
were seaweed hammocks swinging in the
breeze outside. There was a crab neighing
in the sand-stable. Winnie flung herself
into the saddle. 'Giddy-up!' she said.

17

But—**swerve-whoops!** the crab
scuttled sideways. 'Eeeeeeerrrrrr,' said
Winnie, holding on tight. 'Please stop!'
Plop! Off she fell, then she staggered, all
dizzy-dizzy, before, 'Eeeek!' she screamed
because there was a huge eye looking
through the sand-stable door at her.

'Meeeow!' Wilbur was trying to tell her
something urgent.

'What water?' Winnie leaned out of the stable door.

Slop! A wave whacked against the wall of the castle, saltily slapping Winnie in the face.

'Heck in a handkerchief, the blooming tide's coming in!' said Winnie. 'And it's crumbling my walls!'

Wilbur dug, trying to make the moat take water around the castle instead of through it. But the sea is big and powerful, and Winnie's princess castle was small and made of sand.

'Help!' shouted Winnie. 'This castle is collapsing!' The wet walls were sagging and slipping all around her. 'Where's my wand?' wailed Winnie.

But she'd left it out on the sand.

'It'll get washed away! And I'm sinking into the sand! It's sucking me in as if I was a string of spaghetti in a monster's mouth. Oh, Wilbur!'

Wilbur was dig-dig-digging so fast his paws and spade were a blur. But the tide was rising higher and higher, and the castle was crumbling lower and lower. What could Winnie do? Then she saw the lolly stick drawbridge, bobbing on top of the water. 'A raft!' shouted tiny Winnie.

And she heaved herself up onto it in a very un-princesslike way. Suddenly— **slurp!**—a wave sploshed the raft and Winnie out to sea.

'Wilburrrrrr!' shouted Winnie as the raft bucked like a bronco under her. Wilbur pounced. He batted the raft with his paw and sent it—**plop!**—to land on the sand.

Up jumped Winnie. She grabbed her wand. It was huge for her now. But Winnie heaved the wand as if she was a Scotsman tossing the caber, and—**tip-crash!**—it waved as it fell, and Winnie shouted, *'Abracadabra!'*

And there she was, full-sized, again.

'Thank knitted noodles for that!' said
Winnie. The sandcastle was just a sad little
hump in the sand under the water now.
'Let's go home. At least there are no tides
at home,' said Winnie.

24

They flew home to see Winnie's house looking beautiful. The dark clouds and rain had cleared. The sun had come out. There was a rainbow in the sky.

'Just like when Noah's flood was at an end,' said Winnie. 'Oh, I do hope that our flood has gone too.'

The house was still damp. It had squelch-soggy carpets and murky marks on the walls. But the water had gone. Winnie yawned. 'You know, Wilbur, I don't fancy a bath tonight somehow.' She went to clean her teeth . . . and there was the same frog, sitting and looking at Winnie lovingly and pouting his lips.

'Hmm,' pondered Winnie. 'You know what, Wilbur? When princesses kiss frogs they turn into handsome princes. D'you suppose that since I was a princess today it might work for me?'

She was just reaching out a hand to let
the frog step onto it when—**pow!**—
Wilbur's paw batted the frog right out of
the window.

'Oh, Wilbur! Now I'll never know!'

'Meeow,' agreed Wilbur, and he settled
himself onto Winnie's bed.

28

Jurassic
WINNIE

'**Snip-snap!** Oi, wake-up, you sleepy
witch!' Winnie's alarm croc was jumping
around and snapping.

'What do you want, you naggy croc?'
asked Winnie's sleepy slow voice from
under the bed covers.

'Get up, get up, get up! **Snip-snap!**
You're late!'

'Late?' Winnie sat up and looked at
the croc. 'Late for what? Oh pickled

porcupines, in just thirteen minutes
I'm meant to be at the little ordinaries'
swap shop!'

Winnie tugged off her nightie, and
tugged on her clothes so fast she looked
like the contents of a tumble dryer. She
hadn't got time to brush her hair. The
alarm croc tapped his foot and tutted.

30

'I know! I know!' wailed Winnie. 'I'm going as fast as I blooming well can!' She slid down the stairs to save some time. Then she ran into the kitchen where she poured sneereal into a bowl.

'Meeow?' complained Wilbur, his tummy rumbling.

31

'All right, all right!' said Winnie as she tried to put catfish biscuits into a bowl for him at the same time as putting ditchwater into the kettle, but ended up pouring ditchwater onto Wilbur's head and biscuits into the teapot. She put a spoonful of sneereal into her mouth.

32

Pah—spit! 'Yucky-mucky-duckies, why ever would somebody put a . . .' Winnie looked at the soggy card she'd picked from her teeth, '. . . a picture of a brontosaurus in a packet of sneereal?' Winnie threw the card into the bin.

Just then, **Boom boom! Cuckoo! Snip-snap! Brrr!** All the clocks in Winnie's house went off at once.

'Flying fish fingers, we've run out of time! Off to the swap shop! I've got a lovely jigsaw with only three bits missing that I want to swap for something nice.'

In the school hall the children were busy swapping, but they were only swapping cards.

'Jurassic World cards,' explained one of the children. 'If you collect the whole set you get given a book about the dinosaurs who lived then.'

34

'That's wonderful!' said Winnie. 'Oo, where do I get the cards from? I want one of those books. I think some of my ancestors might have been Jurassic.'

'The cards come in packets of Snip Crockle and Poop cereal,' said a child.

'Meeow!' pointed out Wilbur.

'Oh!' said Winnie. 'Do you think that brontosaurus thingy was one of them?'

'The BRONTOSAURUS?' shouted the children. 'That's the card we all need! It's the only card left to find, and nobody's got one. You have to have a complete set by tomorrow to get the book!'

'Oh dilly-doodles!' said Winnie.

'If you give your brontosaurus card to me, I'll give you a velociraptor,' said a boy.

'I'll give you two triceratops!' shouted a girl.

'I'll give you . . . !' shouted all the children at once.

'Heck in a hole, I'd better go and find that blooming card I half ate,' said Winnie.

Winnie rushed home and threw
everything out of the bin, looking for what
was left of the brontosaurus card. But—
eeek!—a rat was just nibbling at the last
corner of the card, chewing the very tip of
the brontosaurus tail.

'Too late!' said Winnie. 'Those little
ordinaries aren't going to be pleased.

Oh, if only I could go back in time and do this morning all over again. Then I'd look after that card. Oo, I know! I'll magic myself to go back in time!'

'Meeow!' warned Wilbur. But Winnie did the most enormous sweep of her wand. *Abracadabra!'*

Time whirled back hundreds of millions of years in a blur, and it dropped Winnie and Wilbur in a strange hot wilderness of plants and insects and smells. 'Er . . . this is a bit further back in time than I had in mind,' said Winnie. 'This might be actual Jurassic times.' Winnie looked around. **Scrunch-munch!**—she heard a noise.

'Hiss!' went Wilbur, the fur on his back sticking up like a toothbrush.

'What is THAT?' said Winnie.

Scrunch-munch! 'Ooooo!' **Thump-bump!** 'Er . . . um . . . uh-oh!' Winnie was looking up at something the size and shape of a lighthouse that had just whumphed down in front of her.

'M-m-meeow!' said Wilbur, as he pointed a claw up and up and up and . . .

41

'Oh, my wormy-woolly-word!'
said Winnie, backing away. Towering
over Winnie and Wilbur was the most
enormous brontosaurus! Down came its
great big head on a long long neck the
length and thickness of a fat tree trunk.
Sniff! went the brontosaurus.

'Er . . . nice Bronty!' said Winnie in a
wobbly voice. She tickled its chin. 'Who's
a very big boy, then? Can I take your
photo, please?' Winnie whipped out her
mobile moan that also worked as a camera.
'Say "cheese!"' said Winnie, stepping back
and back and back to try and get the whole
of the huge dinosaur into her photograph.

'Squeak!' said the brontosaurus just
as Winnie was about to click, making it a
very shaky shot.

'Oh, bother! Please, Mr Brontosaurus, could we just try that one more time?' asked Winnie. 'Thanks ever so. Say "silly sausages!" Mr B!'

'Tweet-tweet!' said the brontosaurus.

Click!

CLICK!

'Ooer, look what saw us!' Winnie pointed to a whole group of dinosaurs who'd gathered to pose for their photos to be taken too. A triceratops, a diplodocus, some little dinomice, and a great big velociraptor. And then . . .

45

Crash! Grrr! Rooaarrr!

Winnie looked over her shoulder.

'Oooer! I spy with my little eye something beginning with 'T'—a great big tyrannosaurus rex! Quick, Wilbur!' Winnie waved her wand. *Abracadabra!*

Whooosh! And they were home.

Winnie printed out the photos, making lots of the brontosaurus one.

'Copies for each of the little ordinaries,' said Winnie. 'Then they can all get the Jurassic book.'

Back at the school, 'Yay, now we've got complete sets!' shouted the children when Winnie gave them the photos.

But, 'Ahem, I think not!' said the Snip
Crockle and Poop cereal man. 'These
aren't the official pictures.'

'They're better than pictures; they're
photographs!' said Winnie.

'Do you think I'm stupid?' said the
man. 'Who ever heard of a brontosaurus
being pink?'

'But they ARE!' said Winnie.

'Nonsense!' said the cereal man.
'There'll be no Jurassic World book for
any of you!'

49

'Oh, Winnie!' shouted the children.

'Huh! The books are as rubbish as a very smelly rubbish dumpy tip anyway,' said Winnie. 'They've got lots of stuff wrong in them. Did you know that a T-rex is bright blue?'

'Really?' said the children.

'Yep. And that a brontosaurus goes tweet-tweet!' said Winnie. 'And . . .'

Winnie and Wilbur had a happy afternoon telling and showing the children some real things about dinosaurs that the people who write books hadn't yet discovered.

The cereal man went home. He looked
at the photo of the brontosaurus. Beside
the brontosaurus was a witch-shaped
shadow.

The cereal man sat and he wondered . . .

A Wedding for
WINNIE

Bing-bong! went Winnie's dooryell.
Winnie opened the door and there stood
her sister Wendy.

Sniff! went Wendy. **Sob!**

'Oh dear!' said Winnie. 'Your eyes are
leaking! Here, have a hankie-pankie. Come
in and have some nice ditchwater tea and a
toasted scrumpet.'

Sigh! Sniff! Sob! went Wendy.
'Oh, Winnie, I get so lonesome, all on my

ownsome. Can I come and live with you?'

'Er...' said Winnie, who really didn't want a weeping Wendy living with her. 'You should get a cat, Wendy. Wilbur's both friend and hot water bottle to me.'

'Meeow!' said Wilbur, carrying in a tray of hot spluttered scrumpets.

'Oh dear!' said Wendy. 'A-a-a-atishoo! Cats make me sneeze! Go away, Wilbur!'

'Mrrow!' Out stomped cross Wilbur.

'Get a dog, then,' said Winnie. 'Or a kangaroo, or a baboon.'

'No!' wailed Wendy. 'Anything furry makes me sneeze.'

'A snake?' said Winnie.

But Wendy shuddered at the thought.

Then she smiled. 'A man might be cuddly!'

'Oo, I've heard that men are more
trouble than cats and dogs,' said Winnie.
'And they have hair.'

'But a man would be romantic!' said
Wendy.

'Well, there's Mr Ball at the garage.
D'you think you could make a catch
out of him? Shall I send him a message?'

'Yes please!' said Wendy.

So, '*Abracadabra!*' Winnie waved her wand. And down flew a pink lovey-dove with a reply note in its beak.

♥ • MR. BALL • ♥
would be delighted
to meet a beautiful
♥ LADY ♥
WITH A VIEW TO POSSIBLE
♥ MARRIAGE ♥

Sigh! 'I feel less lonely already!' said Wendy.

Lovey-doves flapped back and forth,
dropping and collecting notes as fast as
Wendy could read and write them. Wendy
got pinker with every note she read. And
then came one that made her bright red.

'Ooer, he wants me to marry him!' said
Wendy in a wobbly voice.

'Don't you want to meet him before you say "yes"?' said Winnie. 'I wouldn't even buy a toenail clipper without taking a look at it first.'

'But I love him!' said Wendy. **Sigh!** 'Oh, I want a very special wedding. And I want you to be my bridesmaid, Winnie!'

'Me?' said Winnie. She'd gone as red as a boiled bog-berry. 'Really truly?'

Winnie glanced through the window at a
scowling Wilbur and did the thumbs-up.
If she could get Wendy married, then soon
Wilbur could come inside. 'Oh, Wendy, I'll
make it a really really special wedding,' said
Winnie. 'Just tell me what you want!'

Wendy did. She lay on the sofa and
leafed through wedding magazines showing
flowery, flouncy, fantastic weddings.

NEEE OOW!

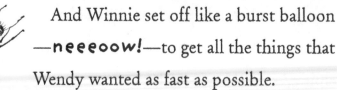

And Winnie set off like a burst balloon
—**neeeoow!**—to get all the things that
Wendy wanted as fast as possible.

'I want lots and lots of smelly-welly
flowers!' **Sigh!** said Wendy.

'Stinkwort and pongberry and wiffle-
lillies,' said Winnie. **Neeeoow!**

Off she went into the garden to snip
and collect smelly flowers and thistles and
dandelions. Wilbur was sulking too much
to help. **Neeeoow!** Back into the house
went Winnie.

'I want a beautiful fruitiful wedding
cake with thirteen layers, and pink icing all
over it!' said Wendy.

'Heck in a hiccupping hippopotamus!'
said Winnie. But—**neeeoow!**—she did
her best—**stir slop slap splatter!**

'I can cook better when I've got Wilbur
helping,' said Winnie sadly.

'Never mind about Wilbur. I want balloons!' said Wendy. So Winnie chewed and blew bubble-gum balloons, getting herself in a sticky-poppy mess.

'I want a dress like a meringue mountain with a long long train,' said Wendy.

So—*neeeoow!*—Winnie did her best with a bed sheet and magic.

Abracadabra!

64

'And I want a Hen Party!' said Wendy.

'What in the wobbly world is one of those?' asked Winnie.

'I don't know, but I want one,' said Wendy.

So Winnie waved her wand. *'Abracadabra!'*

Instantly the room was full of hens, all flapping and pecking and cluck-cluck-squawking! They pecked the balloons—**pop!**—and laid eggs and dropped droppings and . . .

'Oh, if only Wilbur was here to herd them into order!' said Winnie. 'Quick!' she told Wendy. 'Get into the dress and get married before anything else goes wrong!'

Neeeeow! Winnie zipped and glued and pinned and buttoned and stitched Wendy into her dress, then she coupled the train onto the back of it. Then— *neeeoow!*—Winnie did her best with a teasel brush and cockroach hairclips to make Wendy's hair nice.

67

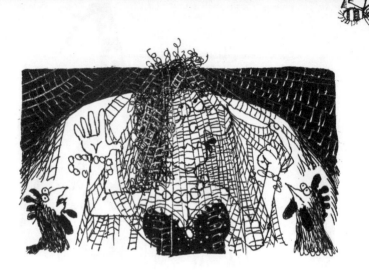

'There,' said Winnie, standing still at last. 'You look as lovely as a little lamb licking a lolly.'

'I want a veil, too!' said Wendy.

'Really?' said Winnie who was too tired to **neeeow!** any more. So she just reached out for some cobwebs, and draped them, spiders and all, over Wendy's head.

'There!' said Winnie. 'You're done.'

'But you're not!' wailed Wendy. 'And really I did want two bridesmaids!'

That gave Winnie an idea. 'You go, and I'll follow in a mini-moment,' said Winnie. 'Wilbur!' she called at the door. 'Come here, Wilbur!'

Swish!—she waved her wand. **'Abracadabra!'** She magicked a flouncy-bouncy dress with hooped underskirts. **Swish!**—**'Abracadabra!'** She magicked another cat-sized one.

'Mrrow!' said Wilbur in disgust.

'Oh, pleeease be a bridesmaid with me!' said Winnie. 'I've been missing you so much!' So Wilbur let himself be buttoned and ribboned. 'Just hold those flowers right in front of your face,' said Winnie. 'Nobody will guess that you're not a little twirly girly!'

The wedding was very special, just as
Winnie had promised. Mr Ball looked a bit
nervous about marrying somebody that
he couldn't see beneath the cobweb veil.
But Winnie had forgotten exactly why
Wendy had said that she couldn't be near
to Wilbur. As the short furry bridesmaid
with a tail sticking out came up behind the
bride and bridegroom . . .

'**A-h-ah-tishoo!**' sneezed Wendy,
and **whoops!** the veil blew right off her
face, showering thistle and dandelion seeds
all around her.

'Ah!' sighed Mr Ball.

'Phewy-dewy-dumplings!' whispered
Winnie. 'He likes her!'

Mr Ball and Wendy liked each other so
much they didn't really notice much about
the wedding except each other . . . which
was just as well, really!

As the new Mrs Ball and her husband
flew off on her broom into the sunset,
Winnie hugged Wilbur tight.

'A man might be more romantic,
Wilbur, but I'm glad that I share my life
with you!'

'Purrrrr!' said Wilbur proudly. He had
forgotten quite how silly he was looking.

73

Nitty
WINNIE

La-di-tiddly-doo-daa!

'What's that music?' said Winnie.
'Ooo, look! The little ordinaries are
dancing around a pole that's as stripy
as my socks, and they've all got ribbons!'

Red, blue, orange, yellow, and green
ribbons were twiddling and weaving
together in a beautiful pattern as the
children skipped around and under
each other.

'Oh, that's as lovely as a baby newt in a nettle flower bonnet!' said Winnie. 'Ooo, please, Mrs Parmar, can I join in?'

'I don't think that's a very good ...' began Mrs Parmar.

But, 'Oh yes, please DO join in!' said a bubbly dance teacher. 'The more the merrier, I say!'

'Brillaramaroodles!' said Winnie. She
grabbed a yellow ribbon and plunged into
the dance, skipping as high as a kangaroo
jumps.

Tiddily jump-bump!

'Hey!'

Diddily slip-trip!

'Ow!'

Winnie wasn't weaving in and out of
the children, and nor was she weaving her
ribbon in with the other ribbons. She was
crashing and tripping and going in the
wrong direction to make such a tangle
of ribbons that it all looked like multi-
coloured spaghetti.

'Oo heck, what a lot of knots!' said Winnie as the music stopped.

'WINNIE!' shouted Mrs Parmar. 'That is NOT how it should be done!'

'No. No, it really isn't,' agreed Miss Bolshoi the dance teacher who had wilted like a dejected daffodil and didn't look nearly as bubbly as before.

'Oh, I'm ever so sorry, Mrs P,' said
Winnie. She looked at the children tangled
with the ribbons. 'Heck in a haddock!'
she said. 'That doesn't look good, does it.
Don't you worry, though. I'll soon sort it!'

'Oh, please . . .' began Mrs Parmar, but
Winnie was already waving her wand.

'Abracadabra!'

And instantly the ribbons came to life,
like skinny bright eels, untangling knots
and then swishing this way and that and
tying the children and Winnie firmly
to the pole. They were soon bound and
gagged by ribbons woven into a tight
criss-cross pattern.

'Mmmnff,' said Winnie, who had purple
ribbon over her mouth.

'A sturdy pair of scissors is the only cure,' said Mrs Parmar. 'And—**snip snip!**—she cut the children and Winnie free.

'That's better!' said Winnie. 'I'd got an itch on my head and no hands able to reach up and scratch it.' **Scrabbly-scratch!** She gave her head a good old scratch now. 'Aah, that's better!'

'But the ribbons are ruined!' wailed Mrs
Parmar. 'We can't possibly do any more
dancing now. You must all go home for
lunch, and I shall have to see if I can buy
more ribbons.'

'Dear, oh dear, oh dear,' said Miss
Bolshoi. 'And people are coming to watch
us this afternoon. Oh dear.'

'Come back at four o'clock sharp,' Mrs Parmar told the children. 'All neat and clean and wearing your best dress if you're a girl and best bow tie if you're a boy. We mustn't let the public down. Oh, I do hope that I can get hold of more ribbons!'

'I'll be there, smart and neat, Mrs P,' promised Winnie.

'Oh dear,' said Miss Bolshoi and Mrs Parmar together.

Winnie and Wilbur went home. *Itch itch* went Winnie's head.

'Hardboiled hiccups!' said Winnie, scratching at her hair. 'What in the whoopsy world is it that's making me so itchy?'

'Meeow?' Wilbur peered and poked at Winnie's hair. 'Mrrrow!' He held up something teeny-tiny and black.

'Whatever is that?' said Winnie.

Wilbur put the teeny-tiny black thing on a bit of white paper. He handed Winnie a magnifying glass.

'It's a lousy louse!' said Winnie. 'Oh, no, I've got nits! Flipping frog flippers,

I'm infested! I must have caught them off those little ordinaries when we were tied tight together!' **Scritch-scratch!** Winnie was scrubbing at her head and dancing around. Wilbur took a step or two back.

'Mrrow!'

'Don't worry, cats don't get lice,' said Winnie.

87

Scratch-scritch! 'Oo, I can't stand this, Wilbur. I must catch them all . . . and then we can sprinkle them on our frogspawn rice pudding for lunch. They may be nice to eat, but they're horrible to be a home to!'

Winnie looked in the mirror, pulling her nasty nest of knotted nitty hair about so that she could try and see what was lurking inside it.

'It's no blooming good,' she said. 'The little lice are black, the same as my hair, so I just can't see them. Oo, I know!' She grabbed her wand. *Abracadabra!*

Instantly Winnie's hair was green.

'Now we can see them!' said Winnie. 'Little black crawly-creepy itch. 'Oo, there's one!' **Snatch!** 'And another!' **Pinch!** 'Can you do the ones round the back of my head, Wilbur?'

It wasn't easy, searching through the tangle of hair, and the searching made the tangles worse.

'It's not exactly neat and smart in the way Mrs P wanted, is it?' said Winnie, prodding her mess of hair. 'I'd better get a better hairdo before we go back to the dancing. *Abracadabra!*'

But none of the styles Winnie tried
looked right, until, *Abracadabra!* . . .

Oo, I like that one! Don't you, Wilbur?
Now, there's just time to get into my
dancing dress, then off we go. I'm sure
Mrs Parmar and Miss Bolshoi will be
very happy to see me.'

Winnie was delighted to be greeted warmly. Wilbur was surprised.

'Oh, welcome, welcome!' said Miss Bolshoi. 'You are just what we need!'

'Really?' said Winnie. 'I *knew* I was a good dancer after all!'

'Dancer? No, no, I don't want you to dance at all. You have a very important part to play in our ribbon dancing, but not as a dancer.'

'Then you mean . . .' began Winnie as she was hustled into the centre of things and the children all surged towards her.

'Remember, take hold of one ribbon each!' trilled Miss Bolshoi. 'Are you ready?' She pushed a button, and the music started.

La-di-tiddly-doo-daa!

And there was Winnie, as tall and stripy as a pole, with ribbons dangling from the top of her head, and the children dancing round and round.

'Oooer!' said Winnie, getting dizzy. She blinked and concentrated hard, and managed not to fall over.

'Oo, well I am quite good at this sort of dancing,' she said.

She was. And when the dance was over, Winnie looked like this.

Enjoy more magic moments with
Winnie AND **Wilbur**